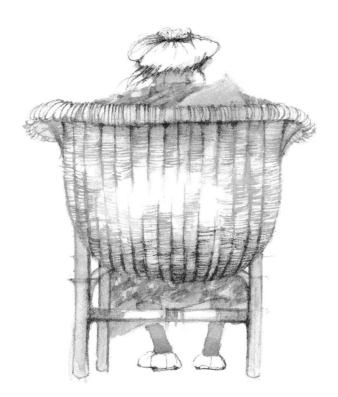

Author's Dedication
For Malcolm

Illustrator's Dedication
For Ana and Kate

Wilfrid Gordon McDonald Partridge

Written by Mem Fox   Illustrated by Julie Vivas

A CRANKY NELL BOOK

Kane/Miller Book Publishers

Brooklyn, New York & La Jolla, California

There was once a small boy called
Wilfrid Gordon McDonald Partridge and what's
more he wasn't very old either.

His house was next door to an old people's home
and he knew all the people who lived there.

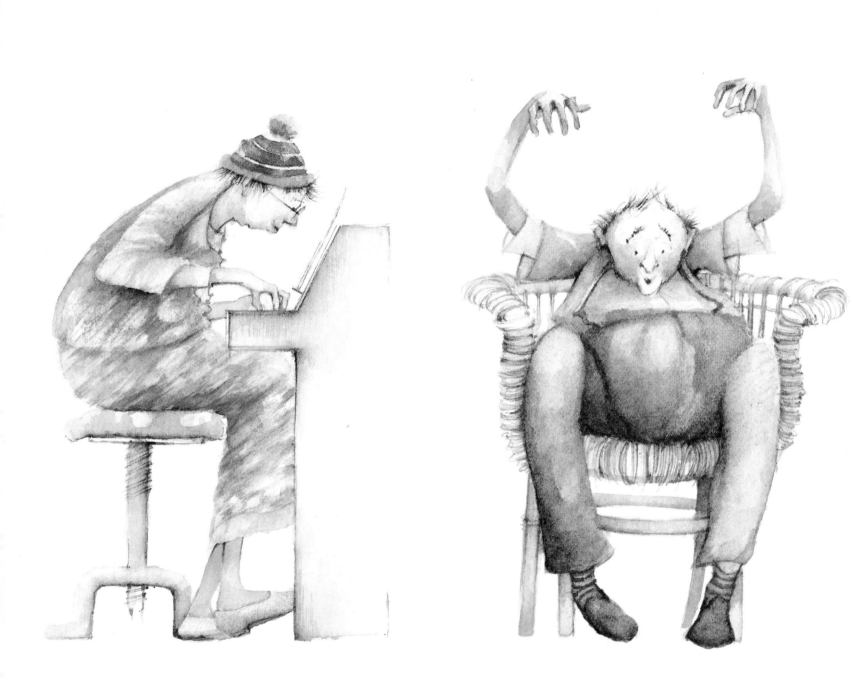

He liked Mrs Jordan who played the organ.

He listened to Mr Hosking who told him scary stories.

He played with Mr Tippett who was crazy about cricket.

He ran errands for Miss Mitchell who walked with a wooden stick.

He admired Mr Drysdale who had a voice like a giant.

But his favourite person of all was Miss Nancy Alison Delacourt Cooper because she had four names just as he did.
He called her Miss Nancy and told her all his secrets.

One day Wilfrid Gordon heard his mother and father talking about Miss Nancy.

"Poor old thing," said his mother.
"Why is she a poor old thing?" asked Wilfrid Gordon.
"Because she's lost her memory," said his father.
"It isn't surprising," said his mother. "After all,
she is ninety-six."
"What's a memory?" asked Wilfrid Gordon. He was
always asking questions.
"It is something you remember," said his father.

But Wilfrid Gordon wanted to know more, so he called on
Mrs Jordan who played the organ.
"What's a memory?" he asked.

"Something warm, my child, something warm."

He called on Mr Hosking who told him scary stories.
"What's a memory?" he asked.

"Something from long ago, me lad, something from long ago."

He called on Mr Tippett who was crazy about cricket.
"What's a memory?" he asked.

"Something that makes you cry, my boy, something
that makes you cry."

He called on Miss Mitchell who walked with a wooden stick.
"What's a memory?" he asked.

"Something that makes you laugh, my darling, something
that makes you laugh."

He called on Mr Drysdale who had a voice like a giant.
"What's a memory?" he asked.

"Something as precious as gold, young man,
something as precious as gold."

So Wilfrid Gordon went home again to look for memories
for Miss Nancy because she had lost her own.

He looked for the shoe-box of shells he had found long ago
last summer, and put them gently in a basket.

He found the puppet on strings which always made everyone
laugh and he put that in the basket too.

He remembered with sadness the medal which his grandfather
had given him and he placed it gently next to the shells.

Next he found his football which was as precious as gold,
and last of all, on his way to Miss Nancy's, he went into the hen house
and took a fresh, warm egg from under a hen.

Then Wilfrid Gordon called on Miss Nancy
and gave her each thing one by one.

"What a dear, strange child to bring me
all these wonderful things," thought Miss Nancy.

Then she started to remember.

She held the warm egg and told
Wilfrid Gordon about the tiny speckled blue eggs
she had once found in a bird's nest in her aunt's garden.

She put a shell to her ear and remembered
going to the beach by tram long ago
and how hot she had felt in her button-up boots.

She touched the medal and talked sadly
of the big brother she had loved
who had gone to the war and never returned.

She smiled at the puppet on strings and
remembered the one she had shown to her sister,
and how she had laughed with a mouth full of porridge.

She bounced the football to Wilfrid Gordon
and remembered the day she had met him
and all the secrets they had told.

And the two of them smiled and smiled
because Miss Nancy's memory had been found again
by a small boy, who wasn't very old either.

First American Edition 1985 by Kane/Miller Book Publishers
Brooklyn, New York & La Jolla, California

Originally published in Australia by Omnibus Books in 1984
Text copyright © Mem Fox 1984
Illustrations copyright © Julie Vivas 1984
For information contact: Kane/Miller Book Publishers
P.O. Box 529, Brooklyn, New York 11231

Library of Congress Cataloging in Publication Data
Fox, Mem, 1946-
    Wilfrid Gordon McDonald Partridge.
    "A Cranky Nell book."
    Summary: A small boy tries to discover the meaning
    of "memory" so he can restore that of an elderly friend.
    [1. Memory—Fiction. 2. Old age—Fiction] I. Vivas,
    Julie, 1947-   ill. II. Title.
    PZ7.F8373Wi 1985   [Fic]   85-14720
    ISBN 0-916291-04-9

Printed in Italy by New Interlitho S.p.A. - Milan

2 3 4 5 6 7 8 9 10